The Brothers Grimm
HANSEL AND GRETEL
illustrated by Sybille Schenker

minedition

Once upon a time,
near a great forest, lived a poor woodcutter
with his two children, Hansel and Gretel,
and their stepmother. When things were good,
they had little enough to eat, but when famine
came to the land, the man could no longer
provide their daily bread.

One night, as he lay in bed worrying, he
sighed to his wife, "What is to become of us?
How can we feed our poor children when we
have nothing to give?"

"You know what, husband," she replied,
"early tomorrow morning we will take the
children into the forest and give them each a
morsel of bread. We will leave them there.
They will never find the way home and we will
be rid of them."

"No, wife. I can't do that. How can I leave my children alone in the forest? Wild animals would tear them to pieces."

"Then we will all die of hunger," said she. And she kept talking until at last he gave in. The children heard what their stepmother and father were talking about. "What shall we do?" wept Gretel. "Don't cry, Gretel. I will save us," replied Hansel.

𝔄t dawn, even before the sun had risen, the woman came and woke the children. "Get up, you lazy things! We are going into the forest to gather wood." Then she gave them each a small piece of bread to eat.

At dawn, even before the sun had risen, the woman came and woke the children. "Get up, you lazy things! We are going into the forest to gather wood." Then she gave them each a small piece of bread to eat.

Then they set off into the forest. As they walked
Hansel dropped breadcrumbs onto the path.

The woman led the children deeper into the forest than they had ever been in their lives. Their father made a fire to keep them warm and the stepmother said, "Just sit there, children, and rest. We are going farther into the forest to cut wood, and in the evening, when we are done, we will come and fetch you."

The woman led the children deeper into the forest than they had ever been in their lives. Their father made a fire to keep them warm and the stepmother said, "Just sit there, children, and rest. We are going farther into the forest to cut wood, and in the evening, when we are done, we will come and fetch you."

Evening fell and deepened, but no one came for the poor children.

They awoke to darkest night. Hansel comforted his little sister, saying, "Just wait until the moon comes up, Gretel. Then we'll see the white breadcrumbs I dropped, and they'll show us the way home."

When the moon appeared, they looked for them, but the breadcrumbs were gone, for all the birds of the field and forest had eaten them. "We will find the way all the same," said Hansel to Gretel, but they did not. They walked the whole night and the next day from the morning till evening, but they did not come out of the forest.

When the moon appeared, they
looked for them, but the breadcrumbs were
gone, for all the birds of the field and forest
had eaten them. "We will find the way all
the same," said Hansel to Gretel, but they
did not. They walked the whole night and
the next day from the morning till evening,
but they did not come out of the forest.

ℜext day was the third morning since they had left their father's house. They began to walk again, but they kept going deeper into the forest. If help did not come soon, they would surely die.

Next day was the third morning since they had left their father's house. They began to walk again, but they kept going deeper into the forest. If help did not come soon, they would surely die.

𝔄t midday they saw
a lovely little snow-white bird sitting on a branch.
It sang so beautifully that they stood still to listen to it.

22 At midday they saw
a lovely little snow-white bird sitting on a branch.
It sang so beautifully that they stood still to listen to it.

When the bird had finished, it
spread its wings and flew off ahead of them.
They followed it to a cottage, where it perched on
the roof.

When the bird had finished, it spread its *wings* and *flew* off ahead of them.
They followed it to a cottage, where it perched on
the roof.

When Hansel and Gretel came closer, they saw that the cottage was made of bread and roofed with cakes, and the windows were made from sugar. "We can have a feast," said Hansel. "I want a piece of the roof, Gretel, and you can have some of the window."

As they began, a gentle voice called from inside:

"Nibble, nibble, munch, munch. Who is chewing on my house?"

And out crept an old woman.
"Oh, my dear children!
Whoever brought you here?
Come in and stay with me.
No harm will come to you."

$\mathfrak{S}$he took them by the hand and led them into
her cottage. There she served them a good meal:
milk and pancakes, with sugar, apples, and nuts
and sweets.

Early next morning as she looked at the children lying there so peacefully with their soft pink cheeks, she murmured to herself, "They will make a tasty meal."

Then she grabbed Hansel with her skinny hand and dragged him out and shut him in to a small kennel. Next she went to Gretel and shook her awake. "Get up, lazybones. Fetch water and cook something for your brother, who is outside in the kennel to be fattened. When he is fat enough, I will eat him."

Gretel began to cry bitterly, but it was no good.

Each morning the old witch crept out to the kennel and called, "Hansel! Stick out your finger so that I can feel how fat it is."

Instead, Hansel held out a small bone. With her dim eyes, the old witch thought it was Hansel's finger. She was amazed that he didn't grow fat at all. After four weeks had passed she was overcome with impatience and would wait no longer.

"I've heated the oven," said the witch to
Gretel, "you crawl in and see if it is hot enough."
But Gretel guessed what she had in mind.
"How can I get in there? It's too small."
"Like this, you silly goose," said the witch.
She hobbled forward and as she stuck her
head in the oven, Gretel gave her a hard push
and slammed the iron door. The witch began
to howl dreadfully, but Gretel ran away, and
the wicked witch was burned to death.

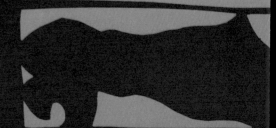

Gretel ran straight to Hansel, opened his kennel, and cried, "Hansel! We are free! The old witch is dead!" How happy they were! They hugged each other and danced about.

Hand in hand they went into the witch's house. In every corner there were chests with pearls and precious stones inside. Hansel put as many in his pockets as they would hold and Gretel filled her apron full.

"Now we must go," said Hansel, "so we can escape this witch's forest." After walking for a few hours they came to a lake.

Gretel called to a white duck:
"Duck, duck. Help Hansel and Gretel.
There's no bridge and no track.
Take us on your little white back."

The good little creature did so, and after they were safely across and had gone on for a while, the forest began to look more and more familiar. Finally, from a distance, they recognized their father's cottage. They began to run, rushed inside, and fell into their father's arms.

The man had not had a single happy hour since he had left the children in the forest. His wife had died. Gretel shook out her apron so that the pearls and precious stones rolled about the room, and Hansel drew out one handful after another from his pockets to add to them. Then all their troubles were at an end, and they lived together happy ever after.

The good little creature did so, and after they were safely across and had gone on for a while, the forest began to look more and more familiar. Finally, from a distance, they recognized their father's cottage. They began to run, rushed inside, and fell into their father's arms.

The man had not had a single happy hour since he had left the children in the forest. His wife had died. Gretel shook out her apron so that the pearls and precious stones rolled about the room, and Hansel drew out one handful after another from his pockets to add to them. Then all their troubles were at an end, and they lived together happy ever after.

The End

minedition

English edition published 2011 by Michael Neugebauer Publishing Ltd., Hong Kong
distributed in GB by BOUNCE! Sales and Marketing Ltd., London
North American edition published 2013 by Michael Neugebauer Publishing Ltd. Hong Kong

Text by the Brothers Grimm, edited and abridged by Martin West
Illustrations copyright © 2011 by Sybille Schenker
Originally published by Michael Neugebauer Publishing Ltd., Hong Kong.
Rights arranged with "minedition" Rights and Licensing AG, Zurich, Switzerland.
All rights reserved. This book, or parts thereof, may not be reproduced
in any form without permission in writing from the publisher,
minedition rights and licensing ag, Zurich, Switzerland.
Michael Neugebauer Publishing Ltd., Unit 23, 7F, Kowloon Bay Industrial Centre,
15 Wang Hoi Road, Kowloon Bay, Hong Kong. Phone +852 2147 0303,
e-mail: info@minedition.com
This book was printed in September 2013 at LEO PAPER PRODUCTS LTD.
Level 36, Tower 1, Enterprise Square Five (Mega Box), 38 Wang Chiu Road Kowloon Bay,
Kowloon, Hong Kong , China
Typesetting in ITC New Baskerville, headlines in Fette Fraktur

A CIP Catalogue record for this book is available from the British Library
Library of Congress Cataloging-in-Publication Data available upon request.

ISBN 978-988-15128-2-6 GB edition
ISBN 978-988-8240-54-8 US edition

10 9 8 7 6 5 4 3 2 1
For more information please visit our website:www.minedition.com